LES VACANCES

Phil Sloman

And this, dear Cate, is
why it is safer and more
joyful to holiday in
well-trod regions rather
than off the beaten track.

Have a fab birthday and
keep on being awesome!

Phil

Published by The Alchemy Press
www.alchemypress.co.uk

LES VACANCES

Phil Sloman

The Alchemy Press

~~ 1~~

The stench of familiarity tainted their room drifting back over twenty years. The decor had changed time and again since their first night together as husband and wife yet all was as it had been. Worn carpet had been replaced by new. The new became worn and was itself replaced and so the cycle repeated. Patterned wallpaper gave way to paint to be covered by wallpaper once more.

She had been the architect of each new style while he had simply agreed without offering an opinion. Their children had both been born in this room. Two mattresses ruined by bloods and fluids spilling from her raw body and seeping into the fabrics beneath. They had hoped to have a third child but it never came to term. Neither of them had spoken of it since even though she wanted to scream about it every single day thereafter, while he could never find the words.

Their children had grown up in the house together, separated by less than three years. Two boys who had played and fought and cried and laughed while being loved and cared for. Friendships had blossomed and vanished as had love interests which were meant to last forever yet invariably frittered away to nothing in three monthly cycles.

The mother and father had seen the world change as their children grew to adulthood. Shillings gave way to sterling. Man landed on the moon promising to colonise the stars only to never set foot there again. The King had died on his throne and Queen had rocked the world. All while the decades took their toll.

And in all that time love had given way to habit and then to indifference.

So here they were today. She had woken first that morning while he slept heavily next to her, his breathing deep and rasping and regular. She lay still, looking up at the textured ceiling with its swirls of paint sweeping across the Artex. The part-formed circles were a distraction, a way to ignore the journey they had ahead of them.

The swirls of paint reminded her of windblown patterns in the yellow sands of Camber where the breeze danced merrily when the tide was low, and the scent of salt and fish was ripe. They holidayed there regularly, squeezing into a too-small caravan, huddling round a three-bar heater when the weather turned foul and the sea breeze coloured their fingers and faces red raw.

All their holidays had been in England where the skies were grey and the food anaemic. It was a Sunday evening when the decision to do something different was made.

The television had been on, the pair of them seated on a sofa which slumped in the middle and had seen better days. Yellowing plastic trays balanced on their laps as they sipped at soup served in white bowls with a single handle to one side, mimicking oversized teacups. Different recipes were glazed on the front of the bowls, each set against a vibrant backdrop of vegetables. Hers was for mulligatawny and his Scotch broth. Instead, their bowls were filled with lukewarm tomato soup, bright orange gunk scrapped from a tin and half-heartedly heated over the stove. She took an uninspired sip at her meal.

John Thaw had been on the television as she continued to feed.

Dip, lift, sip.

Dip, lift, sip.

She watched impassively as Thaw drove around in a beaten-up jalopy which jolted and rattled through the sun-baked hills of Provence.

"We should go there," her husband had said.

She had looked up from her soup, unused to him expressing a view unprompted.

"Where?"

"There." He pointed animatedly, using a spoon coated in viscous orange sauce to emphasise matters. "There, on the telly."

She dabbed her lips with a paper tissue plucked from the hanging sleeve of her cardigan.

"Do you think we could, Frank? I mean, can we afford it?"

"Carpe diem, Elizabeth. Carpe diem."

It was a favourite phrase of his. Carpe Diem. Ever since they had rented that film with the actor who used to be a comedian. Frank had chosen it as part of a discounted deal; rent three films for the weekend, only pay for two. Be kind, rewind. She couldn't entirely remember what Carpe Diem meant but she knew enough to know he had already made up his mind.

"If you're sure, Frank."

"Course I'm sure." He lifted his bowl to his mouth and

took a gulp of soup. His spoon rested on the tray leaving a sticky patch which would need a scrub when they were finished. "Look, the boys are both off to university doing God knows what. Bunking off, most likely. But that doesn't matter right now. This," he jabbed at the screen with a finger this time, "this is what matters. This will be perfect for us. A chance for a bit of sunshine and culture. Or do you fancy another week away in that bloody caravan?"

The truth was, she had. She liked it there down by the coast. Everything was simple and familiar. They had their regular places they liked to go. The owners always left them a little welcome present in the caravan which they didn't have to do and which she thought was nice. And she liked the food. And Norman and June would be there. They were always there. Each year. Familiar faces for familiar times. But she didn't mention any of that. Nor did she push him further on the finances which always seemed stretched whenever she wanted to go out but never when he did. Carpe Diem. Carpe bloody Diem.

She sipped her soup and let her silence imply agreement. If she had voiced her thoughts then perhaps things would have turned out differently in the weeks which were to follow. Perhaps they would have spent another week in Kent with the likes of Norman and June, with food she enjoyed and brisk walks along the beach. But she hadn't said any of that and things didn't turn our differently, and their sons never saw them.

A blur of sunflowers radiated with warmth in the afternoon sun as they hurtled towards Bordeaux in their hearse of a car. The vibrancy of the French countryside was a far cry from the granite sky on the other side of the Channel.

Three times that morning they had gone back into the house before finally setting off: checking and rechecking electrical points were all turned off, making sure they had enough clothes for all eventualities, and leaving a brief note for their cat-sitting neighbours.

Their ferry had been delayed by over an hour. Stormy weather forcing them to sit huddled in their vehicle watching the rain lash against their windshield. Eventually they were given the go ahead to board. The next four hours were spent wandering the on-board duty free and staring through salt-streaked windows as they chewed mouthfuls of limp homemade sandwiches, watching sporadic cargo ships passing in the distance. It was gone two o'clock when they had arrived into the bustle of the French port of Dieppe.

Things were different here. The signs. The language. The side of the road they had to drive on. Frank had taken the first shift behind the wheel, driving while Elizabeth navigated, skirting them to the west of Paris and down the A20. City life gave way to open roads and vast swathes of countryside. The impersonal greyness of the docks relenting to the patchworked contrast of random farmsteads dotted along the motorways. His shirt was clinging to his back with sweat by the time they were halfway down the country, his skin pockmarked from the beaded seat cover he swore helped to relax his muscles. It was a couple of hundred miles later before he took the wheel again.

"I don't know how you can do that without feeling sick," he said, keeping his eyes on the road ahead.

"Do what?"

"That!" He nodded his head in her direction, adjusting the wheel as he veered marginally to the left. "Reading in the car. Always makes me queasy."

"You were alright reading the map."

"Yes, I know, but that's different."

"What's different?"

"You reading like that. I'd be hanging my head out the window by now if that were me."

She snorted in amusement at the imagery, placing the guidebook in her lap to look at him.

"Well, it's interesting. I thought you'd be glad I was showing an interest in where we're going."

"Of course I'm glad," he said, focused on the black tarmac as the sunflowers continued to flank them.

"Well then, what were you complaining for?"

"I wasn't complaining, I was … oh, never mind."

She picked up the book again, flicking through the pages, looking for the section she had been reading. Eventually she found it. Frank kept staring at the road.

"Well, what does it say?"

"What?"

"The book. What does it say?"

"Stuff."

"Stuff? Is that right? Stuff."

"Yes, stuff."

He sighed and stared ahead at the road.

"It says here," she began, "that Pont du Diable … is that how you pronounce it?"

He grunted but she wasn't sure if that was confirmation or the verbal equivalent of a shrug.

"Well, however you say it, it says here that the village dates back to at least the twelfth century."

"Really. That old, eh?"

"That's what it says. And they reckon some parts of it might be older than that."

"You mean like cavemen and that?"

"No, not like cavemen and that. I do wonder about you sometimes, Frank. Too much television, that's what that is. No, it says there was probably a settlement of some kind long before then. Something pagan."

"Like witches you mean."

"Not like witches. I do wish you'd be serious sometimes. Like, I don't know. Like Stonehenge. People worshipping the summer solstice. Things like that."

"Right."

Frank shook his head.

"I'm only reading what it says here. Anyway, the village as it is now grew up some-time around the eighteenth century."

"Is that so? Exciting stuff."

"Look, you asked me what I was reading so I'm telling you. I can stop if you'd rather."

Frank pondered his options and remained quiet. He stayed that way for the next fifty miles, grunting and nodding in appropriate places as Elizabeth continued her monologue. Stories of monasteries rising and falling, of heretics and stakes and fire. Of rebellions and revolution. Tales of abundance and happiness and new beginnings. And within the book there were also lies and omissions and fallacies all designed to gloss over a dark past many had long forgotten. Many but not all.

~~~

Midnight was approaching when they arrived at Pont du Diable, crawling through narrow darkened streets. An occasional light flared here and there from first floor windows as the curious looked to see who was about at that time of night, but the lights were soon extinguished. The road surface was rutted and uneven often petering out into cul-de-sacs and blind alleys. It was with relief that they exited the village to the freedom of the open country road. That relief was short lived.

"Are you sure we're heading the right way?" asked Frank, peering beyond the fall of his headlights, trying to gauge what lay ahead in the darkness.

"I'm just reading the directions you gave me." She held a small torch in her hand. "It says here we drive through the village and the farm is a couple of miles from there."

"Is that all they say? There must be more to it than that."

"That's all it says. Don't you think I'd tell you if there was— Frank, look out!"

Elizabeth grabbed at the steering wheel, lurching the car to the right. Frank slammed his foot hard onto the brakes, the car skidding as the tyres struggled to grip the dusty road. Elizabeth's seatbelt pulled tight across her chest, forcing the breath from her as the car ground to a halt.

"What the hell did you do that for?" There was panic in his voice. Panic and anger.

"Didn't you see her?"

"See who?"

"A woman. There was a woman in the road. Just standing there. She had no clothes on. Jesus Christ, Frank, why would she be naked? Why would was she be there like that?"

"What do you mean a woman?"

"I mean a woman." Elizabeth paused, gathering her thoughts, breathing deeply to calm herself. "An old woman. She was all wrinkled and hunched over… Did, did you hit her? Oh my God, Frank. Tell me you didn't hit her!" Elizabeth was pulling at Frank's sleeve with worrisome fingers.

"No, I … I don't think so. We'd have felt it if we had."

"Are you sure?"

"Of course I'm sure. Go and take a look if you don't believe me."

Elizabeth slumped back into her seat, letting go of Frank.

"I'm not going out there, Frank. You go. You go take a look."

"Why me?"

"You were the one driving. You're the one who hit her."

"I didn't hit anyone!"

"But you don't know for sure."

"For Christ's sake, Lizzie. There's no one there." Frank undid his seatbelt, swearing under his breath. The buckle crunched against the frame of the car as he slammed the door shut behind him. There was a dryness and a warmth to the night air even this close to midnight. Small insects played in the headlights, skittering briefly at Frank's approach only to return seconds later. Frank crouched, slapping absentmindedly at the back of his neck as he examined the road. Nothing. No old woman dead or alive. No damage to the car. Not even any sign of footprints. Nothing.

Sighing, he stood upright, his knees cracking as he did so, and returned to the car.

"Well?" There was an anticipation to her voice. Anticipation and fear of what he might have seen.

"Nothing," he said. "There's nothing there."

"But she was stood right there, Frank. How could she have just vanished?"

"I don't know." Elizabeth waited as Frank considered his words carefully. "Look, Lizzie, I'm tired. You're tired. We're both tired. Perhaps you imagined you saw something out there."

"I didn't imagine anything, Frank."

"Okay, but let's suppose you might have. Look there's no one there. Go outside if you don't believe me."

Elizabeth folded her arms and looked to the passenger window.

"Exactly," continued Frank. "Love, listen. How about we drive to the farm and get a good night's rest. How's that by you?"

Silence.

"Lizzie?"

She busied herself with the guidebook, flattening it out on her lap, breaking the spine, occupying herself with directions to the farm which were little more than blurred shadows in the darkness of the car, the torch lost within the footwell.

"Lizzie?"

She strained to see, bringing the book closer, reaching for the internal light and using what little illumination it gave out. "Drive on, Frank."

"Do you want to talk about it?"

"Just drive, okay. Take the second right up ahead when we get there and then the farm will be straight ahead of us."

Frank shifted the car into reverse. The tyres struggled for grip initially, spinning in the dirt before lurching the car backwards. Frank pressed the brakes bringing the vehicle to a halt.

"Second right? Are you sure?"

"That's what it says here." Her tone was terse.

"Okay. We'll do that then."

Frank pumped the accelerator, revving the engine before taking the car down the country road. They were oblivious to the eyes watching them as they drove away, the rear lights of the car shining red in the darkness.

~~ 3 ~~

Frank jolted awake, banging his knee on the steering wheel, cursing under his breath. It took a moment to remember where he was.

They had driven another ten minutes the previous night before coming upon the farm. There had been no visible lights and no obvious way of attracting their hosts without sounding the horn. Frank had been keen to do so but Elizabeth had persuaded him otherwise, suggesting disturbing the locals at gone midnight might not be the best idea.

They had slept in the car, Frank in the front with Elizabeth laid out on the back seat with a picnic blanket for warmth. Outside, the morning sun hung low in the hazy sky where the early mists were yet to burn away. At night the shadows had given the farm an air of the supernatural. Demons and devils hiding out of sight ready to feast on them in their sleep. Now everything looked different in the daylight, more placid, as the pale light brushed across the courtyard and the surrounding farm buildings.

Frank rubbed his knee. Elizabeth was stirring in the rear seats behind him.

A weather-worn face was staring in through the side window, quizzical eyes peering over a bulbous nose as a gnarled knuckle rapped repeatedly against the glass. "Monsieur, monsieur." The accent was thick and Gallic, the words muffled and indistinct through the glass, but there was no misunderstanding the rapid hand gestures. Frank was met with a verbal barrage as he wound down the window. "Qu'est-ce que tu fais, Monsieur? Qu'est-ce que tu fais?"

"Bonjour." The word sounded inadequate and lumpy coming from Frank's mouth. "Tourists," he continued, pointing at his chest and then towards Elizabeth. "Holiday. From England." He pronounced the words slowly and clearly for good effect. The man's brow furrowed as Frank indicated he was to step back from the car.

"Who is he, Frank?" Elizabeth's voice came out as a cautious whisper, her body still covered with the crosspatch blanket.

"Damned if I know. Probably the owner. Have you still got that guidebook?"

"It's under here somewhere."

"Monsieur!" The tone was forceful.

"Un momento," said Frank, holding up a solitary finger to stave off further admonishment, ignorant of his linguistic failings. The owner watched impassively, arms folded across the barrel of his chest, resting atop a gut fed on dairy, grape and hop.

"Lizzie, the guidebook!" Frank spat the words from between teeth forced into an unconvincing smile.

Elizabeth thrust the battered book in Frank's direction, his fingers snatching it from her a little too eagerly.

"We are looking for, um, La Firm du Gore Nell." Frank held the book out to the man, his fingers pointing at the name of their holiday home. He repeated the name of the gîte once more for good effect. The man snorted through his nose as he grabbed for the guide, the bristles of his moustache twitching briefly. He studied the page with great consideration before looking up.

"La Ferme du Gournelle. C'est la! La!"

A stubby finger pointed back down the road they had driven in from. In the distance Frank could see where they had taken a right turn. Beyond that he could make out a short humpbacked bridge forming part of the route they needed and further in the distance a building which he could not quite make out. The farmer snatched the guidebook from Frank, pointing the battered guide in the direction of the horizon.

"La!"

Frank nodded in realisation. "Okay. Comprendez. Merci, Monsieur. Merci."

The Frenchman grunted, a guttural sound emanating from his chest. Satisfied, he walked back to his farmhouse, muttering all the way as he threw a dismissive hand over his shoulder.

~~ 4 ~~

Gravel crunched under dust-whitened tyres as they pulled into the courtyard. Chickens scattered across the ground in a flurry of muck and feathers, running haphazardly until they found an overturned water trough to shelter behind. Dogs barked excitedly from a farmhouse to their right, the cacophony becoming clearer once the car's engine fell silent. If they had taken the left turn last night they would have been here within minutes, a short drive to the humpbacked bridge and the farm beyond. Frank sighed inwardly as he opened his door and set foot outside the vehicle.

"Hello," he shouted, half-clinging to the safety of his door. "Is anyone there?"

He waited, watching the surrounding buildings for any sign of movement or other indication of life beyond the chickens and the dying noise of the dogs.

The farm was an apology of architecture. Most looked to have been pieced together with whatever was to hand at the time. The farmhouse echoed the masonry of the low walls marking the boundaries of the farmstead; large chunks of local stone ripped from the ground and sealed together with mortar and mud. The farmhouse's roof sloped irregularly, covered in moss-speckled thatch woven from straw and reeds. A small wooden fence surrounded the house, corralling a sweep of grass bordered by flowers, which Frank assumed passed for a garden of sorts. Open stables sprang up to the left of the farmhouse, beds of straw covering the ground inside with the rear walls obscured by bales of hay skewered with pitchforks. An antiquated tractor sat under the shade of the stables. It was compact, more tires and engine than anything else, with a seat barely the size of a frying pan to sit upon. A white plastered building, taller than the farmhouse, dominated the rear of the property. Its angled roof blocked the rising sun, casting a dark shadow across the top end of the courtyard.

Elizabeth leant out of the car window. "Any luck, Frank?"

"Nope. Nothing. Can't see anyone as yet."

Elizabeth eased herself from the car. She stretched, her arms reaching to the sky as she tried to shake the journey from her bones. Bending, she brushed the creases from her dress. As she stood again, a glint of light caught her eye.

"Frank, what's that over there?"

Frank followed the direction of her arm.

Without waiting for invitation, Elizabeth was already halfway across the courtyard to investigate.

"Wait up!"

Elizabeth ignored him. It felt good to let the blood flow, to get some movement in her legs and, after all, what was the worst that could happen. It wasn't as if they were trespassing. They had paid to come here.

The glint became obvious the closer she got. A single brass bell fastened to the gate post caught the morning sun. It looked like it had been taken from the cabin of a small fishing boat, the kind used to let the port hands know the catch was safely in the docks. A knotted length of rope hung from the bell, its weight swaying gently back and forth in the light breeze. A small rectangle of cardboard was nailed to the post with three words painted on the card in faded black. Elizabeth crouched to get a better look.

"Sonner pour l'attention." She ran the unfamiliar words round her mouth, her hand resting on the post. "What do you think that means?"

"Damned if I know. Something about attention?"

"Should we ring it?"

"I guess so. Either that or stand here all day waiting for someone to show up."

The rope felt coarse in her grip, woven by hand using techniques long forgotten by many. Elizabeth's first swing was lacklustre, a timid motion which barely raised a sound. The second was bolder, a rapid clatter demanding attention, setting off the dogs in the farmhouse once more. It reminded Elizabeth of the dinner bell from her schooldays, used to call the children in from playtime, the schoolmistress swinging it with gay abandon.

"Well?" asked Frank, expecting Elizabeth to have all the answers.

Elizabeth ignored him, shading her eyes as she peered around the courtyard, looking for any sign of life. For a moment she thought she saw movement in the upstairs of the farmhouse, a twitch of a curtain raised and then hastily replaced as if the voyeur had been caught in the act. Elizabeth took a step towards the building to get a closer look.

"Hoy! Qui es-tu?"

Elizabeth turned to the voice behind her. A young woman was walking toward them from the white building, bath towels folded in her arms. Long dark hair cascaded down below her shoulders. Her step was quick and her face impassive. It was Frank who answered first, continuing his full repertoire of Englishman abroad, his voice loud and the words forced, his hands flung around in gestures meant to convey meaning but lacking in any.

"English. Tourists. My wife and I. We have a reservation."

He was met with a bemused expression.

"Parlez vous Anglais?" continued Frank, the default position of the exasperated linguaphobe.

"Yes, oui. I speak your language. Perhaps better than you."

Frank ignored the slight, glad to have someone he could finally communicate with.

"We made a booking with you. For the gîte."

"You are the Dixons? Yes?" Frank nodded. "We were expecting you last night."

"We got lost," said Frank, exchanging an accusatory glance with Elizabeth.

"It happens. These roads, they all look the same to you outsiders." She let the word hang there, setting the boundaries between host and guests. The dogs were quieting down in the background. Elizabeth wondered if someone inside the house was calming them. The same someone who had watched from the window. "Monsieur, Madame, excuse me. It is early and I am forgetting my manners. I am Madeleine. You must be Frank and

Elizabeth, yes?"

"Yes, spot on," said Frank, eagerness creeping into his voice. Elizabeth remained quiet. She looked back to the upstairs window and then to Madeleine.

"Bien. Well, welcome. Please, come with me. Follow. We will get your luggage soon."

Elizabeth glanced back at the house one final time before joining the others.

~~~

Madeleine gave them a brief tour of the facilities within the gîte. The building had been rebuilt in recent years so it could be repurposed as accommodation for visitors. The downstairs were light and airy, and split into two main rooms. The first was an open dining area. A large oak table dominated the centre of the room, bedecked with crockery, flowers and tall white church candles. Even with the size of the table, there was ample room for a small sofa and television in the corner, and a bookcase nestled into a recessed alcove; "part of the original building" as Madeleine had said.

The rest of the downstairs were taken up by a small kitchen area with cooker, sink and fridge. Fitted cupboards completed the room and were part-filled with provisions Madeleine had left them for an evening meal. The fridge would be refilled every day with fresh eggs, butter and milk from the farm. Any further supplies were to be gathered by them from the village they had driven through the night before.

The floor above them only covered two thirds of the space, leaving a balcony overlooking the downstairs. "I think you, especially, Madame Dixon, will appreciate this." Madeleine led them upstairs, ascending an elegant wooden staircase, the sound of their footsteps echoing off the stone walls.

Elizabeth let out a gasp of delight as they crested the top of the stairs. Perhaps things were going to be better here than Camber. A circular stained-glass window was set in the centre of the rear wall spilling coloured light across a handcrafted double bed. Delicate reds and yellows intermingled with bolder greens on the white bedsheets which were themselves covered with a sprinkling of rose petals. A white porcelain jug and ceramic bowl stood on a washstand against the north wall. To the left a matching bath sat mounted on four carved feet, copper pipes running from its base to the wall, deep enough to fit the pair of them with ease.

Madeleine draped the towels she was carrying over the curved edge of the bath.

"I trust all is to your liking."

"It's perfect," purred Elizabeth, the previous night's ordeals forgotten.

"Beats a week in Camber, eh?" said Frank, almost reading her mind as he put his arm around her shoulder, hugging Elizabeth into his body.

"Oh, Frank, it's delightful."

It was only when they went to get their luggage that Camber Sands seemed a lot more attractive.

~~ 5 ~~

"Well it didn't say anything about murders in that book of yours. This must be where they buried the evidence."

"Frank!" snapped Elizabeth.

"What? I'm only joking." He gave Elizabeth a look. "Anyway, it's obviously not recent. I mean, look at them. Must be from back in the dark ages."

"The dark ages? I am sorry, I don't understand." Madeleine was standing with them in the shadow of the gîte, goose pimples pricking up along her bare arms. She had taken them on a tour of the farm to show them the places they were allowed to go. The courtyard, the gîte, the farmhouse when invited. Nowhere else. The stables were out of bounds. As was a small gathering of outbuildings behind them. For their own safety, she had said, with the farm being a working one.

It had been Elizabeth who had spotted the stones poking up behind their home for the coming week and insisted they take a look.

"The dark ages. When they still had knights in shining armour and burned witches at the stake."

Elizabeth couldn't be sure but she thought their hostess' face dropped for a second, the veneer of hospitality replaced by something else. Something unfriendly. And then the smile returned.

"Ah, yes. Witches and bogeymen. Like you see at the cinema. Amusing tales, yes? Good for getting children to eat their vegetables."

"But these are graves," interjected Elizabeth. "They're not from some film. They're here. Right here! Why did no one tell us about this when we booked?"

Madeleine looked from Elizabeth to the ground. A succession of mounds protruded from the soil. Grass and wildflowers covered the lumps, exaggerated undulations which could have been explained away in any number of ways. Except for the gravestones.

"The people are dead. As your husband says, they have been dead a long, long time. They will not hurt you."

"That's not the point…"

"Honey, it's okay." Frank put an arm around her shoulder. There was a quiver to her body as he pulled her closer. She pushed him away.

"Many, many years ago, this place," Madeleine indicated the rear of the gîte with a sweep of her arm, "it used to be our monastery. Even before the village was here. These are simply the graves from back then. The monks who lived here. Little more than dust beneath the earth."

"How did they die?" Elizabeth's words were abrupt.

"I think it says it here, Lizzie." Frank was peering at one of the graves, trying to read the weathered letters carved into the stone. "This definitely says die."

Madeleine gave a little laugh, one which could easily have been considered charming yet, to Elizabeth's ear, it dripped with condescension. "Ah, Monsieur Dixon, it says Dieu, not die." Madeleine placed a hand on his shoulder and guided him in closer to the gravestone. She traced the letters with her finger. "See the U here. But I see how you can be mistaken. Dieu is God. The whole thing says 'Dieu sait qui a tort et a péché'. In English it means 'God knows who is wrong and has sinned'."

"So they were murdered?"

"Old age, Madame Dixon. Old age. I can assure you that not everything you imagine is true. These were men of God. What would they have to fear?" Madeleine moved to face Elizabeth, her hand resting on Frank's shoulder a moment longer than seemed natural. "We all live long healthy lives here. The weather, the air, the food. All good for the health. Nothing has changed in hundreds of years. The monks, they went to sleep and never woke up. It is sad but it is life."

"Nothing to worry about then, right, Lizzie?" Elizabeth could have slapped Frank. If he was going to take sides then he should be on hers.

"Well, I still don't like it. Sleeping next to corpses. It's not my idea of a relaxing holiday."

"Madame Dixon, I assure you we have guests here all the time. We have never had any complaints. If you do not bother the dead then they will not bother you." Madeleine reached out a hand in a gesture of friendship. "Please, come. Let us get your luggage. Then you can sit down, relax, and enjoy yourself. I shall even bring you a little something extra for your meal as way of an apology. After all, you know what they call a meal without wine?"

Elizabeth reluctantly let Madeleine take her hand, allowing her to clasp it in a way she found overly familiar. "Breakfast, Madame Dixon, breakfast. And the sun is long past midday."

~~ 6 ~~

"Look, let's see the week out, love."

Frank shovelled another forkful of steak into his mouth. The meat had been part of the welcome package along with some wild mushrooms, garlic, and big fat tomatoes from the farm. Frank had never learnt to cook beyond the art of blackening sausages on a barbecue so culinary duties had fallen to Elizabeth. He raised a glass of red wine to his lips to wash down his meal. Elizabeth sat taciturn across from him, her cutlery in hand. She had barely touched her food though her wine glass stood almost empty to her right.

"I mean," Frank continued, "you seemed quite interested in all that historical stuff on the drive here."

Elizabeth gently laid her cutlery down beside her plate. Her response might as well have come from between gritted teeth.

"That was before I realised we were going to be living in it. And at no point did it mention us staying in a graveyard." She reached across and grabbed the half-drunk bottle of wine from the table and topped up her glass, filling it as close to the brim as she dared.

"Don't you think you should go steady on that, love? You know how your head gets in the morning after one too many."

"I'll do what I like, thank you very much."

"Well, don't blame me when you're feeling delicate

tomorrow."

Elizabeth took a large mouthful of wine, swallowing it back, not bothering to taste it before pouring herself another glass.

"That would be the least of the things I'll be blaming you for."

Frank let his cutlery clatter onto his plate.

"And what the hell do you mean by that?"

"I mean that we could be having a nice time with Norman and June right now rather than sitting here where nobody understands us and…"

"Madeleine understands us!"

"And who else apart from her?" Elizabeth was standing now, her hands clenched, fists planted firmly on the table. "Maybe the dead monks? What about them? Shall we go and dig them up and ask them? And don't think I haven't seen the way you've been looking at her either, prancing around after her like a lovesick teenager."

"You're just being stupid now."

"Oh, I'm the one being stupid, am I? Tell me it's not true."

Frank paused for breath, his face a mask of confusion. This was meant to be a nice week away yet here they were on day two at each other's throats.

"Look, love," he said, choosing his words with caution, "why don't we call it a night before we both say something we're going to regret?"

"I'm not the one with anything to regret!"

"I know, I know." His hands were raised, fingers stretched out as he tried to calm the situation. "I tried to do a nice thing for both of us and clearly I screwed up somewhere along the line."

Elizabeth gave him a look.

"How about I clear away the dishes, love, and maybe we head on up for an early night?"

"Do whatever the hell you want. I'm past caring."

The neck of the wine bottle fitted comfortably in her hand as she stormed away to flop onto the sofa in the corner of the room.

~~~

She didn't know how long the face in the window had been staring at her like that – milk-filmed eyes stretched wide above a thin mouth pulled into a moon-touched grin. Wisps of grey hair grew like filaments of fungus across a paper-thin crown of mottled skin. Lumps of puffy flesh hung below aged eye sockets, jaundiced from a lifetime of cheap nicotine. The voyeur might have been attractive when she was young but youth had parted company with her many years ago.

Elizabeth saw a familiarity to the face as she stared back. Not the type associated with that of a long-absent friend or family member, or even the anonymous people she saw in the street every day on her daily outings to work, the people she would nod her head at in recognition without ever knowing their name. This was the familiarity of a face half-glimpsed, dredged up from recent memories, incorporeal and fading.

A brittle fingernail tapped at the window with metronomic rhythm. Tap, tap, tap. Tap, tap, tap. The lunatic grin became more of a smile as the tapping continued, clumsy and awkward, an attempt at friendliness from features trying to grasp the concept. The tapping ceased and a finger pointed to the catch on the inside of the window. That smile again, yellowed teeth showing as the thin lips parted. A simple message in the dead of night. Let me in. Let me in. Please, please, oh please let me in. Don't be scared of the hairs on my chinny chin chin.

Elizabeth pushed back the bed covers, looking to Frank for reassurance but he was nowhere to be seen. She sighed. Once more not by her side when it mattered. Never mind. She would deal with it.

There was a warmth to the floorboards beneath her bare feet as she slipped from the bed. Damp footprints followed in her wake, faint impressions of moisture left where the wood sweated, insubstantial vapours of steam drifting up from the floorboards.

It was only now she wondered how the hag could be staring in through the upper floor window. A ladder, perhaps? But why?

"What do you want?" she asked the wind as much as the hag.

The metronomic rhythm started up again in reply. Tap tap tap. Tap tap tap.

The room was becoming misty. The walls themselves weeping as she came closer to the window. Beads of perspiration crested her brow.

Tap tap tap. Tap tap tap.

"What do you want?" The words were shouted this time, delivered with a force which Elizabeth felt would tear her throat open.

Tap tap tap.

And now the wood at her feet was warping. The

grooves between the boards were widening, showing glimpses of the ground floor. She thought she could see Frank there, his naked body shimmering in the glow of an open fire, the sag of his buttocks plain for the world to see. And beneath him was a woman with rich bronzed skin. Her nails raked across her lover's back as he thrust deep inside her. Talons drawing blood which ran down his ribs in thick rivulets of life. And the fire around them grew, a conflagration consuming the lovers and the building. Elizabeth rushed to the window on pain-filled feet as the oak-coloured floor blackened and smouldered. The face on the other side of the panes writhed in rapturous delight, cackling as Elizabeth fought with the catch to get outside to safety even as the fire tugged at her nightdress.

Reality broke.

Elizabeth awoke gasping in darkness, her body cramped in the confines of the sofa. The night air was hot and close. Her clothes were damp and clinging across her armpits, back and chest. It was a different heat to the sporadic waves they experienced back at home. This a dry heat. Suffocating. Each breath was laboured making her throat constrict involuntarily. Her tongue felt furry and engorged in her mouth as she ran it across her teeth. Her head ached with a dull wrath and she could still taste the residuals of the cabernet, rich and plumy, yet metallic now, like a corroded battery.

Elizabeth stumbled her way to standing, trying to command feet which had no intention of cooperating. Her temples throbbed at the rapid change in altitude forcing her to slump down into the forgiving cushions of the sofa. Elizabeth stood a second time, tentatively, fighting the heat and her own personal traumas. The kitchen was a few feet away and all she needed to do was put one foot in front of the other. One foot in front of the other. One foot in front of … one foot. Just one foot.

She veered to the left, clutching at the doorframe to the kitchen, breathing deeply as she fought to regain a semblance of composure. The kitchen was a dizzying sway of motion, no one surface seeming to occupy a single place for longer than a second. Elizabeth closed her eyes. It was a full two minutes before the confusion subsided.

It took three steps and several deep breaths to stagger from the entrance to the sink. Elizabeth grabbed for the ceramic rim, missed, grabbed again. She stood like that, hand gripping the side for comfort, her feet firmly on the floor, for what could have been seconds or hours, letting the wave of nausea wash over her. The tap squealed in agony when she eventually turned it on as the pipes drew water up from the depths of the earth. She let cold water course over her tongue as she put her mouth to the flowing water. It tasted chalky but she didn't care, lapping it up as if she hadn't drunk anything for days. Her face was coated in a fine mist when she was finished, her hair peppered with small droplets of water. She stood upright, breathing deeply, trying to regulate her self-poisoned body. It was then that she noticed the lights outside in the distance.

There was only one at first, a solitary flame fluttering in the darkness as the summer breeze plucked at it, the torch held aloft by a lone figure.

There were others; their features were obscured, lost

within heavy cowls, their bodies covered in long dark robes which robbed them of shape and substance. They walked slowly, seemingly unaware they were being watched as they continued up the slopes. The light grew as Elizabeth watched on, the hills appearing gently to catch fire, a gradual progression of warmth and colour painting the ground a subdued orange.

More and more torchbearers appeared, in ones and twos to begin with, then swelling in number, joining their leader to form a procession of lights flickering in unison across the crest of the hill. They slithered across the countryside, the passage of flames like an engorged snake swollen from a kill, bulging at the centre before tapering away to the rear.

And at the centre there was something held aloft.

Or someone.

It was hard for Elizabeth to make out the detail from this distance amidst the unreliable light. To her eyes it looked like some kind of platform supporting a mound of white rags, a bier being carried on the shoulders of many. The walkers stumbled, jolting their burden, adjusting their step to stop from collapsing the procession, for it couldn't be considered anything else. Something limp and fleshy flopped into view, dangling loosely as the procession continued. One of the gathering hurried to cover it up.

"Frank! Frank!" Elizabeth's vocal cords were tight, her words more squeaks than the cries of urgency she had intended. She swallowed deeply and shouted again. "Frank!"

Elizabeth counted the seconds, the pounding in her

head keeping time with her, stretching seconds to an eternity. And yet again he wasn't there for her. When she needed him. Always when she needed him. "Frank," she screamed, pent-up tears burning hot in her eyes, her throat raw. "Frank!" It was then she heard his voice over the balcony.

"What? What is it? Do you know what time it is?"

"Frank. I need you. I need you here now." Her voice quivered as she fought back her fear. The dream, the procession, the arm... Whose arm? It was all too much.

"Christ, Lizzie, are you all right, love? What's happened?"

"Quickly!"

Bare feet thudded on the wooden stairs, Frank's gut wobbling as he ran, his robe still half-undone as he stumbled into the kitchen. The tiles were cool beneath his bare feet but he didn't notice. He only saw his wife trembling, her face broken with emotions. He stepped forward and pulled Elizabeth into him, feeling the warmth of her against his chest.

"I'm scared, Frank. I'm really scared."

Frank looked down into the face of his wife. There was a panic there he recognised. It had been there when they had rushed to the hospital all those years ago, cramps in her stomach, a dark stain spreading round her crotch. He had seen it again when their youngest had fallen through the ice, crossing a winter pond he had been warned about, egged on by his brother, shivering when Frank had pulled him to safety. And it was here again now.

"It's okay, love. I've got you." His words were soft and gentle. "Tell me what happened."

"I saw them, Frank. I saw them. Out there." She pushed away from him, pointing at the window. "Fifty or more. All carrying torches. And, Frank. Oh God, Frank. They were carrying a body. A body, Frank. Why would they be doing that? Do you think they're coming for us? What if they come for us?"

"Calm down, love." He sighed without thinking. "Now tell me, who, who's coming?"

"Monks, Frank. The goddamned monks. I saw them. All of them. You must have seen them." He stood there silently, watching her, looking for words he didn't have. He wanted to tell her everything would be fine. But he'd told her that before and been wrong, oh so wrong, so he'd never said it again.

"Let me take a look outside, love. Eh?"

He gently pushed her to one side, guiding her out of his way. His reflection looked back at him from the darkened glass of the window. He leant forward, feeling the stretch through his legs as he pushed up onto the tips of his toes, perching his gut on the edge of the worktop to get a better view.

"Out here?" he asked, pointing.

She nodded.

"What is it I'm meant to be looking at?"

"I told you, Frank. Didn't you listen?"

"I did listen, love. But there's nothing out there. Tell me again, what am I supposed to be looking for?"

"The lights, Frank. The fucking lights."

Frank spun round, anger in his face. Elizabeth held her ground.

"There are no *fucking* lights out there. And how dare

you swear at me. You're the one who woke me up in the middle of the night. Remember, or are you still drunk?"

"Don't take that tone with me." It was Elizabeth's turn to shove Frank out the way. "Those lights…" She halted mid-flow, staring out the window. The hillside was in darkness save for the moon and stars. She took a step closer to the sink hoping to see something, anything, from the window beyond. "I don't understand. They were there. Just like I said they were. You've got to believe me."

"Goodnight, Elizabeth. I'm going back to bed."

And with that he left her alone, pausing only to look at the two upturned bottles of wine on the living room floor before marching up the stairs.

7

"How's your head?"

Elizabeth didn't bother to reply. Instead she watched the countryside through the car window as they drove towards the village. Frank had let her sleep in until well after ten. Even then sleep had felt fleeting.

Her dreams were filled with images of monks with burning brands preparing to burn down the gîte while the two of them slept inside. She had run downstairs to stop them, carrying the bowl from the washstand, the water inside sloshing onto the floor around her feet. The door to the gîte had been forced open from outside, the lead monk standing there, torch in hand. She had acted from instinct, flinging the water, drenching the flame and the monk.

Perhaps her subconscious had hoped for a Wicked Witch of the West moment, to see the monk and his clan crumple in a heap to the floor as the water melted their aged flesh. Instead she woke up screaming as the monk pulled back his cowl. Even awake, his hollowed-out eyes and the dark slit for a nose were all she could see before her.

The journey to the village seemed so simple now in the daylight. A short drive to the bridge then beyond and on to a crossroads. From there it took less than ten minutes to reach the village outskirts. The houses here were built close together, packed tightly as if there was a need to huddle together for safety. Each house was a two-up two-down affair where the front doors opened straight on to the street. Narrow passageways led off the main road between irregular gaps in the housing.

Locals ambled through the streets, crowding the roads without a care for traffic. As it was, the Dixons' was the only vehicle that day as they crawled toward the main square. Frank beeped his horn.

"Frank, don't," snapped Elizabeth, but it was too late.

Villagers made way, shuffling to the sides of the street, their gaze fixated on the car and its passengers. There were no smiles. No friendly welcome to these new arrivals. Only a glum scrutiny passing from one face to the next. Elizabeth was certain one among them was the farmer from the previous day and all she could think was, it was a long way from Camber.

"Frank, perhaps we should go back to the gîte?"

"Don't be ridiculous," he said, pulling the car into the side of the road. "You said you wanted to get out, so this is us getting out."

He slammed the car door behind him as he stepped out, waiting for her to join him in the warm morning sunshine. Ahead lay the main square, a water pump at its centre, the handle warped and broken. Someone had left flowers at its base, drying and brittle. Fallen petals skittered amongst the dust in the gentle morning breeze. Ramshackle shops lay to the right of the square, converted from the houses which lined the street. Flaked paint clung tenuously to faded shop signs, the wooden boards warped from year after year of hot summer sun. Villagers congregated outside, busy in conversation, holding bags of fresh breads and meats ahead of their afternoon meal. They hushed when they saw Frank. Standing. Unasked for. He half-raised his hand, ready to wave, then stopped, self-conscious, thrusting it back into this pocket.

"Lizzie," he pushed her name out through gritted teeth, forcing a smile for an audience who didn't care. "Are you coming?"

She didn't answer him. It was hot. Too hot now they had stopped driving. She unbuttoned the top button of her dress. And then another. She needed some air but not on his terms. They had come to see the church. That's what today was about. Getting out. Seeing the sights. Being tourists in a strange land. The guidebook had described the church as "of historical importance", built sometime back in the fourteenth century long after the monastery had first opened its doors. The stained-glass windows were meant to be of significant importance though the guide had omitted any more detail than that. Its spire crowned above the surrounding buildings. Like a sundial, it cast its ever-moving shadow across the square before evening ushered everything into darkness. Looking now, she could see the coolness of its shadow cutting across the far side of the square. How she would welcome being there, out of the sun. Yet.

"Fine," said Frank, leaning into the car. "You stay there then."

A dust cloud swirled around Frank's heels as he stormed across the square. The locals watched on like vultures, weathered faces impassive, their conversation forgotten. He pulled open the door to one of the shops, not caring which, and strode inside. Elizabeth didn't care either way. At least now she could…

Small hands clamoured at her window. A swarm of small children all no older than ten years of age pressing up against the glass, trying to get a better look at her, sun-kissed faces all smeared with a thin layer of mud and perspiration.

"Mademoiselle, mademoiselle." Small palms patted at the window, each one desperate to get her attention, to have the foreign lady look their way. They reminded her of when her boys had been that age, full of mischief and wonder, rather than the grown men her sons were now. One day she hoped her sons would have children themselves. Nanny Beth had a nice ring to it. A girl would be nice too. And she would be there whenever she was needed and not when she wasn't, which would be rare. But that was for the future. Her sons had years ahead of them before grandchildren were an option for her. But at least she could pretend for now. If only for a moment.

She shooed the children back with a flick of her hand, repeating the action until they had all backed up enough for her to open the door. It closed behind her with a gentle thud as she stretched herself into the fresh air. It felt good to have the gentle breeze brush her face and her legs. Smiling, she crouched down level with the children, their eyes bright and curious.

"Bonjour." Her pronunciation was nervous making the word sound more like a question than a greeting. What was she doing? She should have stayed in the car. In England.

The pack parted and a blonde-haired girl stepped forward, smaller than the others, wearing a blue dress in need of repair, the stitching fraying in several places. She clutched a wilted bunch of flowers in her hand, reds and yellows, all limp and battered. Elizabeth wouldn't have been surprised if they had been snatched from a neighbour's windowsill or found dropped along the roadside.

"Dix francs," she said, thrusting the flowers out in front of her. Elizabeth looked at her blankly.

"Dix…"

"Dix francs," repeated the girl. She struggled to hold up ten fingers by way of translation without dropping the limp bunch, hugging the blooms to her chest with her forearm and crushing the stalks further.

Elizabeth chuckled. It felt a long time since she had laughed out loud. So that was what they wanted. Money. Elizabeth shook her head and held up three fingers.

Eight fingers this time. A counteroffer. Elizabeth responded with four.

Eight again and a little curtsey.

Elizabeth sighed and looked in her handbag, fishing out her purse. The coins and notes might as well have been Monopoly money to her for all she recognised them. The words EGALITE, FRATERNITE, LIBERTE repeated across the metal discs. The number ten flashed in front of her, a circle of gold surrounding a silver coloured centre. She plucked it from her purse, the metal catching the sunlight as she held it out for the girl. The child watched Elizabeth warily, cautious of some trick, looking around for moral support from her friends. With one hand she held out the flowers for Elizabeth, gingerly reaching out with her other for the money. Nail-bitten fingers plucked the coin from Elizabeth's grip. At the same time the flowers were flung to the floor at her feet.

Then they scattered. The girl and the rest of the children running off into the distance, happy to have achieved their aims, all thoughts of offering change never once crossing their minds. It didn't matter to Elizabeth. There was something infectious about their impishness. She smiled as they disappeared from sight. Her calm vanished as rough fingers grasped her wrist.

"You should not give them money. It only encourages them."

The words were whispered into her ear, the stench of alcohol and urine plucked at Elizabeth's nostrils as she looked around, afraid to see who or what had hold of her. Cornflower blue eyes peered out from a mess of hair. Untamed whiskers, wiry and nicotine-yellowed, framed a muck-smeared face which might have been attractive once.

"Get off me!" Elizabeth yanked her arm away, desperate to be free.

"Leave while you still can." She could taste the cheap wine on his breath as he ignored her cries. "I'm warning you."

"Allez, allez!" A portly man came running from the church across the square, the lip of his cassock flapping around his ankles. Small round glasses perched on the bridge of his nose, one finger pressed firm against them to keep them in place. His run was ungainly, more of a quickened waddle impinged by his clothing. Still, it was enough, and Elizabeth was grateful for it as the pressure on her wrist released.

"They're after me," Blue Eyes whispered. There was a look of pity in his expression. "They'll come for you next."

Then, with a sneer at the vicar, he was away, moving with far more speed than Elizabeth would have thought him capable of.

8

Elizabeth's skin pimpled as the vicar ushered her into the cool earthiness of the church. History oozed from the thick stone walls. School trips in the depths of Sussex as a child sprang to mind, venturing to places like Bodiam and Battle, traipsing round ruins with her friends, listening to the teachers espousing historical footnotes she had never had cause to use in later life.

Limpid pools of blues, reds and greens cascaded across the floor, brightening the rows of pews where coloured light spilled in from large stained-glass windows mounted in the surrounding walls. Each window was magnificent, depicting evocative scenes unfamiliar to her, a story unfolding as she looked from one image to the next.

The first images showed peasants dragging rock from the local hills while men on horseback watched on. Buildings rose from the rich French soil as the sun shone down. The church the tallest of them all. The church spire, haloed with light, was surrounded by cavorting angels celebrating its erection high into the heavens. The scene shifted over the next few windows, moving beyond the village, men and women crossing the bridge, the river churning underneath them, burning brands in hand, repeated in the windows on the other side of the church. Men in robes – *monks, not more monks*, thought Elizabeth – watched from the monastery, their faces portrayed as bitter and spiteful, all twisted and deformed. Even so, there was a beauty to the imagery. Each piece of glass chosen with the care of a master craftsman and placed with purpose. Elizabeth could almost hear the cries and smell the flames as she moved to the final window dominant behind the altar.

Red and orange tongues of fire lapped at the base of the monastery as thick smoke rose from its rafters. A crowd of villagers watched on, some with pitchforks and scythes in hand. One face stood out from amongst the mob. A face wrinkled and grey … and familiar. Elizabeth stepped forward to take a closer look…

The vicar coughed behind her.

"I am sorry." The cracked Gallic tones broke her attention, bringing her back to the here and now. "He is…" The vicar paused, searching for the right word in English for his newfound visitor. Instead he opted for sign language, tipping his hand to his mouth as if holding a glass. Elizabeth looked puzzled, still lost in the past.

"The man on the street…" He pointed towards the large wooden doors, now closed to keep anyone from getting in unannounced … or out.

"Thank you," Elizabeth blurted, realisation dawning.

"De rien." He waved a hand dismissively. "But tell me, are you okay? Did he hurt you?"

Elizabeth shook her head, subconsciously rubbing her wrist where she had been grabbed.

"May I?" The vicar held out his hand, inviting Elizabeth's trust. She offered him her wrist. His hands were warmer than she had expected, and there was a delicacy to his examination, squat fingers probing with care. Her injury was more tender than she had realised, still red around the wrist though the skin had not been broken. He smiled at her with his moon of a face.

"Nothing serious, no? You have been lucky this time."

Elizabeth smiled back although lucky was the last thing she felt.

"Please, sit." He indicated a pew to her. "I will get you some water. Oui?"

"Um, oui."

His cassock flapped around his ankles as he scurried towards the transept. He looked back once before exiting through a side door.

Elizabeth waited for his footsteps to quieten before she rose. The stone slabs were smooth beneath her feet, warped from centuries of passage from the faithful and the pious. She imagined the building filled with the masses seeking forgiveness and hope, yet here she was alone, too old for hope, perhaps. Had they ever found what they were looking for? She didn't know. The only answer she had now was her footsteps fracturing the silence reminding her just how small she was in this house of God. Ahead lay the altar decked with candles and a depiction of the Holy Christ on the cross. She wondered if she should ask for forgiveness. For her and for Frank.

Soft colours dominated the front of the church, illuminated by the late morning sun. Dust motes danced in the tinted light like lost spirits seeking pleasure one last time. Elizabeth exhaled in awe. The stained glass was richer close up, the orange and red of the flames even more radiant. The characters were alive here. She was convinced the villagers moved each time she looked away, raging with their makeshift weapons. Undoubtedly it was a trick of the light, the sun blocked momentarily by fleeting wisps of clouds unseen from within the church making the figures move; and yet…

Accompanying the scene were words engraved in the stonework beneath the lip of the window, gouged out of the wall centuries before. Elizabeth strained her neck forward, squinting as she tried to read the letters hidden within the shadows. She could see the word *Dieu* and perhaps another said *qui*. The rest were lost to her.

The door to the transept opened.

Elizabeth jumped at the hand on her shoulder, almost knocking the glass from the vicar's grip.

"I'm sorry." Her words stuttered, guilty as if caught in the act. "You frightened me."

"It is nothing. Do you like this?" He pointed at the scene above them.

Elizabeth nodded.

"Dieu sait qui a tort et a péché," he said, reading the inscription. "Old words. I don't know the English for it."

"God knows who has wronged and has sinned," whispered Elizabeth, the words barely escaping her mouth.

"Pardon?"

"God knows who has wronged and has sinned. That's what it says at the farm. It's on the graves. At the gîte. Our gîte."

Elizabeth could feel the vast building closing in on her, the temperature rising as her face flushed and her throat constricted. She needed to get out. She needed fresh air.

She needed to be anywhere but here.

She fled for the exit, barging past the vicar, the glass tumbling from his hand, water spilling on to the polished stone beneath creating dark patterns on the ground. He stared after her, mouth open wide. She almost stumbled twice in her desperation to reach the exit, grabbing at the pews to steady herself. The brass ring of the door was heavy, far heavier than she remembered. But then it had been him who had let her in. She twisted the handle one way and then the other, fighting with it before she felt a give to the lock.

Clean summer air assaulted her as she pushed open the heavy church doors, bursting into the blinding sunlight of the square. The vicar stood helpless behind, watching from the doorway as Elizabeth spilled down the stone steps, her feet unreliable as she stumbled towards the centre of the square before collapsing into the waiting arms of her confused and relieved husband.

~~ 9 ~~

"We heard you were attacked in the village today."

Madeleine stood in the doorway to the gîte. They hadn't been back more than an hour when Frank had heard the knock at the door.

Confusion was writ large all over Frank's face. His mother had always said he was an open book, easy to read. His father had simply told him never to play cards for money.

"How did…"

"It is a small place. And we also have telephones."

Madeleine gave him a knowing wink, smirking as the beginnings of a smile formed on Frank's face.

"Of course," he said, forcing an unconvincing laugh.

"We wanted to make sure you were okay."

"We?"

He hadn't considered a "we" before. Guilt forced him to look over his shoulder. Elizabeth had taken to their bed. Exhaustion from the previous night and the stress of the day had proven too much for her. It had been Frank's suggestion she take an afternoon nap to try and regain some of her verve.

"Mother and I."

Relief flooded through Frank as he gave one last look inside the gîte before returning his full attention to Madeleine. He leant against the doorjamb in what he hoped was a casual manner.

"Your mother. I didn't realise your mother lived with you."

"Yes, this is her farm. All this—" she swept her arm round in a semi-circle "—was built by my mother and father. Sadly, my father is no longer with us."

"I'm sorry to hear that." Frank placed a reassuring arm on Madeleine's shoulder. Instead of flinching she stepped in closer.

"Thank you. It was a long time ago." She looked in Frank's eyes, letting him lose himself in their burnt coffee darkness. "Perhaps you could come for dinner this evening."

"I'd like that." He leant in closer, drawn into a fantasy he had only dreamed about until now. He could feel her warm breath on his face, could smell the hay rich scent of her hair.

"You and your wife." She placed a gentle hand on his chest, casually reasserting the distance between them.

"Yes, of course," he spluttered, the spell broken. He was back to being an overweight man of a certain age.

"We say bien sûr over here, Frank."

"I'm sorry?"

Madeleine giggled at him. "Oui, bien sûr. It means, *yes, of course*. Now we have that agreed, I shall be on my way. Please pass my best wishes on to your charming wife."

Frank watched the sway of their hostess' hips as she headed back across the farmyard. His cheeks flushed as she looked back over her shoulder. "Eight o'clock sharp, Monsieur Dixon. We look forward to it." She didn't miss a step as she looked back to the farmhouse, leaving Frank to stare after her, his cheeks growing redder and redder.

~~~

The inside of the farmhouse was far more spacious than Elizabeth had expected, decorated in a simple rustic fashion. Madeleine had welcomed them at the door, embracing the Dixons like old friends before encouraging them into the lounge. The smell of cooking meat drifted through from the kitchen, mingling with the musty smell of dog, which clung to the furniture and curtains. A wooden table dominated the centre of the room. It was large enough to comfortably sit at least eight people although only four places had been set this evening. Fresh flowers stood proud in a vase in the middle of the table: yellows, reds and purples, adding a splash of colour to the room. Two earthenware jugs sat either side of the bouquet, one filled with wine, the other with water, their swan necks pointing elegantly to the ceiling.

Madeleine pulled out a high-backed chair for Elizabeth, the oak legs scraping on the tiled floor.

"Please be seated."

"Thank you," muttered Elizabeth as Frank sat down next to her. It had taken a lot from Frank to convince her to come this evening. She didn't see why they had to mix with the owners. On another day she might have had the strength for the argument but today had taken its toll as had the wine from the night before. In the end it had come down to spending an evening on her own in the gîte or here with Frank and their hosts.

"Wine?"

"Bien sûr," said Frank with the enthusiasm of a five-year-old who has learnt a new trick.

Madeleine's measures were generous, each glass filled

close to the brim. Frank raised his in tribute to their hostess, a large sense of bonhomie spreading across his face.

"Merci, Madeleine. Merci!"

"De rien, Frank. It is a pleasure. Now, if you will excuse me, I shall go help mother bring the food from the kitchen."

The door shut gently behind her as Madeleine left the room.

"Well, you could make an effort," sniped Frank once he was certain they were alone. "We are guests in someone else's home, remember?"

"Of course I remember. I may not be as pretty as little miss perfect out there but I do have a brain in my head."

"And what is that meant to mean?"

"Merci, Madeleine, merci. It's pathetic. You know she's probably laughing about you to her mother right now."

Frank's lips pursed as heat flushed his cheeks.

"Well, at least I get something resembling friendliness from her which is more than can be said—"

The door to the kitchen swung open halting Frank mid-flow.

"How is everything?" Madeleine stood holding a tray of breads and side dishes. Unspoken words passed between Frank and Elizabeth. "I take it the wine is to your liking?"

Elizabeth raised her glass to their hostess and took a drink.

"Bien, Madame Dixon. I am so glad. And now we have the bread and some pieces for our main course. Frank, would you help me please?"

"Of course."

"And mother is on her way with the star of our show. All is perfect."

Frank took the tray from Madeleine, placing it at the head of the table. Steam rose from a bowl of boiled potatoes as he lifted the lid and placed it to one side.

"Smells lovely," he said.

"Smells lovely," muttered Elizabeth in mimicry, not caring if anyone heard her. She drank deeply from her glass.

"Maman, nous sommes prêts," called Madeleine, encouraging her mother to join them.

Irregular footsteps drummed a rhythm from the other side of the door, one foot compensating for the failings of the other. Step, drag, step. Step, drag, step. Then a pause. Waiting on the other side of the entrance to the room. Adjusting the grip on whatever is being carried. A grunt as a back is pushed against the timber of the door to tease it open. Shuffle, shuffle, shuffle as the steps are now taken backwards. A misaligned spine and protruding shoulder blade, both covered in an ill-fitting black dress, greet the room. The head is bent over as the woman concentrates on the load being carried, but what little of her crown that can be seen from behind is sparsely covered with hair. She turns, her pace slow as the one foot again adjusts for the other. And Elizabeth's world collapses.

Her hands take on a mind of their own, knocking her wine glass across the table, red liquid spilling over the rich wood and seeping into the cracks as a scream escapes her lips. Dogs barking can be heard from the outside yard, the frustrated song of creatures hearing distress, dogs who are chained up themselves and can do nothing about it. But Elizabeth doesn't hear the dogs barking or the concerned words from Frank and Madeleine. All she can do is stare wide-mouthed at the face from the road, the face from the window, from the church, from her dreams.

Of Madeleine's mother.

~~ 10 ~~

"Lizzie, are you okay?" Frank was at her elbow, propping her up, concern in his eyes.

"I'm sorry. I really don't know what came over me."

"Do you need to lie down? I thought you were going to faint."

"No, no. I think I'll be alright."

"Here, Madame Dixon, some water." A ceramic cup found its way into her hand. "Please take your time."

Elizabeth sipped at the water tentatively. Three faces were staring at her. The fool, the whore and the hag. Three faces watching as the blood slowly returned to her washed-out face. Steam rose from a haunch of meat at the head of the table, now removed from the tray the hag had been carrying. Pink-tinged juices seeped from the cut onto a bone-white plate, encouraged by a carving knife and fork plunged deep into its crown.

"Perhaps it was the excitement of the day, Madame Dixon?" Elizabeth's brow furrowed as Madeleine continued. "The man in the village, the one who attacked you."

"I'll be fine," she said, more assertively this time, desperate to have the attention away from her. It was all coincidence and she was tired, her mind playing tricks on her. The mother was just an old lady. There were probably a dozen women who looked like her within the surrounding area alone. A dozen hags. A dozen burners of the pious. Elizabeth took another sip of water.

"Are you sure, Lizzie?"

"I'll be fine." Her cup slammed onto the rough wood of the tabletop, punctuating her words as spots of water speckled the surface where red wine had spilled so recently.

A look was shared between the three.

"Perhaps we should go?" ventured Frank.

"No, we're staying. You wanted us to come and we're here now."

Frank looked from Elizabeth to Madeleine then back again.

"Please stay. Maman and I have spent many hours preparing the food. There is too much for us to eat alone."

"There you go, Frank. She wants us to stay."

"Bien. It is settled then. Monsieur Dixon." Madeleine indicated his seat with an outstretched hand. The conductor directing a tune of her making. "Maman, la viande."

The hag shuffled to the head of the table, that irregular step making her bob as she moved, mesmerising Elizabeth as the old lady took up the carving knife and fork. The meat resisted, puckering momentarily before releasing the metal from its bulk. The hag plunged the tines back into the joint further from the centre, the carving knife firm in her other hand. She grunted.

"Maman would like us to pray. Please, do as I do. It is tradition. Before we serve our offering, we must give our thanks."

Elizabeth thought the word strange. *Offering*. Perhaps it was simply a poor translation from the French, yet it jarred with her.

Madeleine sat, planting her elbows on the table with both hands clasped together and her eyes closed. Frank followed suit without question even though the last time he had entered a church with any religious intent was the day they christened their youngest. It had always been Elizabeth who had been the believer. Her who wore the symbol of her faith. Her who followed the teachings of her Lord so as not to burn in the fires of Hell. Elizabeth waited, eyeing the mother before falling into step with the others.

Elizabeth listened in darkness as the old woman presented her prayer. The words meant nothing to Elizabeth, delivered in a hoarse voice, forcing her to strain to hear the unfamiliar syllables. Her mind drifted, lulled by the prayer and eased by wine. Images flitted through her imagination. Villagers gathered in front of the gîte, though the building looked different to now. The walls were rough and unpainted. Simpler. She thought she could hear shouting from inside the building though she couldn't tell whether it was in warning or in fear. Fists fell upon the doors from the outside, the villagers pounding on the entrance, demanding their will be done. Then the noise subsided. The crowd parted as a procession of burning torches made its way towards the building. Each torchbearer stopped before the entrance to spit upon the doors as they dropped their burning brand at the base.

Time collapsed.

The building was now in flames. Bloodied palms slapped wetly at windows, sandaled feet kicking out the glass in desperation. The first body fell from the top floor, brown robes flapping in the air like a wind-caught rag before thumping into the ground with a sickening thud. The second body came straight after, followed by another and another and another. Enfeebled limbs were raised from the ground with futility where the monks lay winded and broken, begging help from their tormentors. They prayed sense would prevail, that the reality of the situation would calm the flame lit faces of insanity surrounding them. But there was to be no salvation.

Elizabeth watched on in terror, not wanting to believe what she was seeing. She tried to close her eyes, to tear herself from the carnage. Except she couldn't. These were not her memories. She watched helpless as the first villager fell upon the broken men. Over-eager hands wrenched at malformed limbs, dragging and pulling, yellowed teeth biting deep into warm flesh, ripping and tearing, lips coated red. She saw all this, and more, and all she could do was scream and scream and scream.

The room around her was silent. Everyone was looking at Elizabeth. Again, those eyes. Those accusing staring eyes. All three of them watching, judging – the fool, the hag and the whore. Why were they all so fascinated with her?

"You were screaming, Elizabeth," Frank offered in explanation.

Elizabeth looked from face to face. "Something ran over my foot. A mouse or something. It was nothing." The lie came more easily than she would have thought she was capable of. The mother shrugged and began to carve the meat. Elizabeth could not tell whether she had understood the English or was bored with the sideshow.

Frank and Madeleine exchanged another of their intimate glances but nothing more was said.

"More wine, Madame Dixon?"

Madeleine reached over and refilled Elizabeth's glass to the brim, not waiting for a response before doing the same with Frank's. The hag cut deeply into the joint. Her forearm quivered as she gripped the fork tightly, the skin on her knuckles stretched paper-thin, loose folds of flesh hanging from her forearms. Thick cuts of meat fell one on top of the other as the knife sawed back and forth. Madeleine rose to help her mother, plating the slices and passing them to their guests. Elizabeth sipped at her wine as Frank piled vegetables on to their plates. Her temples tightened as the alcohol took effect. Something was wrong. Dreadfully so. As if Frank and she were part of a game with rules she didn't understand.

"Please, eat," encouraged Madeleine, fork in hand.

Elizabeth picked up her cutlery. It felt alien to her as if someone else was holding it instead. Her mind wandered, trying to piece together her thoughts. Maybe Frank was right. Maybe it was all in her head. After all, what had actually happened to her beyond a scare outside the church? But the lights. The people on the hills. What about them? No matter what Frank said she couldn't have imagined them. She bit into the meat.

The texture was coarse. She'd had similar meat in her youth when her father bought cheaper cuts from the butcher, taken from older beasts. Scrag harvested from scrawny malnourished creatures with nothing left in their lives of drudgery other than the bolt gun at the slaughterhouse. Those cuts had ended up in stews, boiled far longer than necessary until something stringy and gelatinous was presented in their bowls. She swallowed.

"Why were there people on the hills last night?"

Frank kicked her under the table. Elizabeth glowered at him in return.

"People?" Madeleine put her fork down.

"It's nothing," said Frank. "A little too much to drink yesterday."

"It was not nothing." Elizabeth might as well have snarled. "There were people on the hills. And they were carrying someone. I saw them with my own two eyes."

"Madame Dixon. Elizabeth." Madeleine pronounced the name Lizabet. "Perhaps it was fireflies you saw. We get them this time of year. Very, very pretty but often we have people confuse them. They are like your, what's the phrase, your will-o'-the-wisp. Phantoms of the night. Nothing more."

The mother watched from the head of the table.

"It was not fireflies! There's something out there in the hills. You know there is." Wine-stained spittle flecked Elizabeth's lips as she continued to press. She didn't care whether she offended their hosts or not. She wanted the truth. She wanted to know she was still sane.

"I think we should go, Lizzie. I think we should go now." Her arm was soft in his grip as he reached for her, fingers clamping down on her bicep. He'd never grabbed her like that before. Not once. Now here, in a stranger's kitchen… She pulled away from him, wrenching her arm from his grasp. What was happening? She didn't understand. She wanted to scream at him, at all of them, to make this all go away. Her head felt like it wanted to explode.

"Why? Why won't you believe me? After all our years together? Why? Can't you see they've got the Devil running wild here?"

Frank stood dumbfounded.

"Madame Dixon, I think your husband is right," said Madeleine. "Perhaps now would be a good time for you to leave."

Elizabeth scanned the room. An audience of three with her the centre of attention. Each face focused on her. Judging. It was then she knew was alone. All alone without anyone to fight her corner. Was that the game? Had she lost so quickly and so tamely? If so, what now? Elizabeth's shoulders sagged in resignation as Frank put an arm around her, with her barely aware of what was happening, guiding her towards the door on reluctant feet. They were almost at the door…

"A long time ago others said the Devil walked here."

Elizabeth turned.

It was the hag who had spoken. Her words were slow, demanding attention as they hovered in the air. "But there are more dangerous things than the Devil who walk this earth."

"What the hell are you doing?" Frank watched as Elizabeth whirled around the upper level of the gîte like a woman possessed, flinging clothes haphazardly into suitcases.

"What does it look like? I'm packing, Frank. I'm done. I'm not spending another minute in this godforsaken place."

She had stormed from the farmhouse, not wanting to hear any more of the old woman's words. Spots of rain had started falling as she staggered towards the gîte with Frank chasing after her. Thin elongated droplets which became heavy and bulbous in the time it took to cross the courtyard and fumble with the locks. The deluge fell hard and fast, drumming a cacophonic stanza repeatedly on the roof as they argued downstairs. The windows wept as recriminations were flung back and forth between the married couple. Words better left unsaid. About things from when they were younger which neither of them could have controlled. Words like *fault*. And *your*.

It was shortly after that Elizabeth began to pack.

"Get out of my way!" Elizabeth clutched the hastily stuffed suitcase in her hands. The travel one. Small enough to carry what she needed without weighing her down. A dishevelled Mary Poppins waiting for Mr Banks to come to his senses. All she needed was a spoonful of sugar to help the bitter, bitter pill of deception go down.

"No." His voice was quiet, nearly lost beneath the tumult of rain outside.

"I mean it, Frank. Move."

"No." He crossed his arms in an attempt to exert his authority. "We'll go in the morning. I promise we'll go in the morning. But not tonight. Not with you in this state."

Elizabeth considered her options. Perhaps he was right. Perhaps tomorrow was best after a night's sleep. But he had said the same yesterday and they were still here. Still with the hag and the whore. She took a step closer, seeing if he would move. Nothing.

The suitcase caught Frank a glancing blow to the temple. Elizabeth almost toppled down the stairs as she overbalanced. Only the downward trajectory of the luggage hitting the floor prevented her from doing so.

Frank staggered to the wall of the gîte, leaning against the brickwork for support. Wet sticky fingertips came down from his forehead as he tried to assess the damage. Elizabeth didn't wait for a second invitation to run.

Frank was recovered by the time she reached the bottom of the stairs. He stood on the upper landing hollering obscenities at her, vile words he had never used in all their married time together. She wondered how many of those words had been pent up over the years, hidden, unspoken, and how many were born from this evil place.

The storm outside raged on, defying her to leave, testing her resolve. It didn't matter how loud it became, her fear of staying outweighed the terrors of the elements. Death lived here and all she knew to do was to run away as far and as fast as she could. She stumbled to the entrance, Frank's footsteps thundering down the stairs behind her. What would she do if he tried to stop her forcibly? She didn't know. She doubted she could overpower him but she would try. Another blow with the suitcase. Perhaps. Her hand clasped the handle, ready to fling the door open.

She stopped.

Knocking echoed around the downstairs. A torrent of blows descending upon the door from outside, one after the other with the insistence of a machine gun. It sounded as if the timbers were going to burst under the desperation of the assault.

Immobilised by doubt, Elizabeth let her hand drop from the handle. Frank was upon her, barging her to the side. He was ready to do what Elizabeth wasn't, ready to fling the door open to greet their hosts.

~~ 12 ~~

Frank blinked in surprise. A raggedy man was silhouetted against the doorway, grabbing at the doorframe for support as the elements raged around him. Puddles were forming where he stood with the wind driving rain through the opening to the gîte. Thin clothing clung hungrily to him. Frank thought he could make out individual ribs pressed tight by the damp cloth. Lightning flashed in the night sky illuminating stark features. Dirty blonde hair clung to a face tangled with a mess of beard which gave weight to his jawline. Matted streaks of dried black gunk ran from an off-centre nose down to parched, peeling lips.

"Aidez-moi." The words were forced. Croaked. Quiet. The sigh of an unoiled hinge. Elizabeth screamed as the man collapsed into the building, falling even as Frank tried to catch him. The back of his shirt was savaged and covered in blood. Weeping red lines etched out an irregular ladder either side of his spine. His buttocks were covered by a snatch of cloth, barely hanging low enough to maintain any long-lost semblance of dignity. Frank looked down at the man. He felt bile rising up his throat as he followed Elizabeth's gaze, seeing what had caused her to scream.

"Quick, let's get him to the sofa." Frank's words were urgent, using action to mask his panic. Frank rolled the man over, trying to force helping hands beneath the man's limp body. Elizabeth now saw the face as the man twisted, eyes staring into nothingness, saliva mingling with blood and rainwater. A raving lunatic warning her of doom.

The square seemed an age ago. Those cornflower blue eyes now filled with pain and suffering. She looked from his face, down his torso, to below the loincloth. Guilt forced her to avert her gaze. Her mouth salivated, remembering the chewy texture of their evening meal. The joint the width of a man's thigh.

"Lizzie, don't just stand there."

Fifty years of poor living had taken their toll on Frank. Even now he was struggling to lift the man from the floor to the sofa. Elizabeth stepped forward and put a forearm under the vagrant's armpit, his solitary leg thumping across the floor as they dragged him to the sofa. The man's eyes opened. Panic took over, his body writhing in their grasp until he remembered where he was.

"La voiture? Ou?" He looked at their blank expressions. "Car. Your car. Where is it?"

A tremor of pain passed through his body. His breathing became sharp, drinking long draughts of air through clenched teeth. His fist thumped the sofa arm. "Where?"

"It's in the courtyard," spluttered Frank. "Why?"

Elizabeth didn't wait to hear the answer. The car keys were already in her hand.

"Do you really need to ask? Look at him, Frank. Just look at him." Her stomach turned again. "Who do you think did that to him?"

"You." The vagrant pointed at Elizabeth. "I warned

you."

"What's he talking about, Elizabeth?"

"After me, they come for you. I told you this."

"Wait, is he the man who attacked you?"

"Not now, Frank! I need to think."

"Now, you are too late." He chuckled to himself. "So, so late."

"Lizzie....?"

"Frank, we've got to get to the car. We've got to go now."

She didn't wait for further comment. There were no other options. There was still time to get away before they came for them. There had to be. And even if there wasn't, surely the three of them could overpower the old women and her daughter. But what if they couldn't?

Elizabeth ran to the kitchen, throwing the car keys on to the dining table. She pulled at drawers with both hands, wrenching them open as she hunted for weapons. She cast aside the smaller knives, discarding them with out of hand. It was the bigger knives she wanted, the ones she could drive deep into anyone who got in their way.

"Lizzie!" Frank's voice carried through to the kitchen. "Lizzie, you need to come here."

Elizabeth ignored him, cutlery tumbling around her.

"Lizzie!"

"I'm coming, Frank."

She had what she wanted. A black handle with a long wicked blade. This would be the new game. The one where she got to write the rules. She didn't know if she could really, truly use the knife, but she was ready to try if she got the chance.

Elizabeth strode back to the table for the keys but never picked them up. Frank was pointing at something beyond the open doorway. Elizabeth followed his line of sight. She put the knife down flat on the table. It would be no use to them now. She might get one of them. Maybe two. But no more. They were there. Outside. All of them. The hooded torchbearers, the children, the mistress and the hag. All standing in the open courtyard, dogs straining on their leashes, as the rain fell and their torches burned bright.

~~ 13 ~~

The dogs had rushed them first, jumping high to knock them down, teeth snapping and biting and tearing at the three of them. Then robed figures had followed, strong hands dragging them from the gîte. They had tried to fight back, biting, scratching, kicking, lashing out indiscriminately. Elizabeth had caught someone in the eye, the flesh soft as her finger gouged deeper. There had been hope for a moment as Frank had broken free, running, his feet slipping on the rain-soaked ground, looking for a gap in the crowd. But it had all been futile in the end. There was no gap. There was no last-minute miracle to save them all. Instead, they had been wrestled to the ground, four villagers to each of them, and held down in the wet dirt.

Elizabeth had thought they would die there and then, gutted and fed to the dogs. Instead the hag had given instructions to her daughter, watching from the edges of a malformed circle as Madeleine approached the victims.

In her hand Madeleine held a small potion bottle, bulbous at the base and tapered at the neck. She had crouched down next to Elizabeth, marginally hitching up her dress as she did so. Madeleine had set the bottle to one side, nestling it in the softened ground.

"We were hoping to do this over dinner, Madame Dixon. A little something in your wine." Madeleine had brushed Elizabeth's hair away from her face. "It would have been easier that way. For all of us."

Elizabeth had spat at the Frenchwoman. Her reward had been a stinging slap across the cheek. Rough hands had grabbed her hair, pulling hard and forcing her chin to arch up to the sky. Another hand grabbed her exposed chin, forcing her mouth open while someone pinched her nose. Liquid had splashed onto her tongue before she realised what was happening, the taste bitter like burnt coffee granules. She'd wanted to retch as it ran down the inside of her throat but couldn't. A hand had clasped her mouth shut while fingers squeezed her nostrils tight. She'd swallowed, coughing uncontrollably as the hands holding her head were released. The world had swayed around her, human shapes blurring and contorting into brushstrokes of colour. The last thing she had seen was the face of the hag leering at her, yellowed teeth enlarged and eyes which burned red. And then darkness had claimed her.

~~~

She awoke to a bruised sky, the rains stopped for now, carried upon the shoulders of people she didn't know. People who wanted her dead. Pain flared everywhere. Lactic acid building in her shoulders, both arms twisted at an irregular angle to force her palms face out. Her ankles and wrists were tied with coarse lengths of rope, her body bound to a makeshift crucifix. Red welts were forming where the rope and wood fought against each other and her skin. Pain flared deep in her belly where the acrid liquid still burned. She assumed the same was true for Frank and the stranger, the three of them bound and bleeding. It was only now she realised she didn't know the vagrant's name.

With effort she could move her head left or right, letting her cheek fall onto the neck of the cross. The hillside jolted in her vision with the movement of the mob, uneven ground forcing those who bore her weight to slow their passage. Isolated flashes of lightning illuminated the surrounding countryside, highlighting how far from hope and salvation the trio were. In the distance she could see the gîte, its white exterior prominent within the confines of the farm. She thought back to yesterday which seemed so long ago now, standing in the kitchen, the heat of the room confusing her, watching people on the hillside from the window. People carrying something. Something human. Had it been real. Perhaps. Another victim to be vanished – she couldn't see how this evening would end in any other way. Or perhaps it had been a premonition. A vision granted to her of the future. An inevitable future she had never asked for.

Flaming torches flanked her on either side. Orange light played across her features highlighting the lines and wrinkles of a simple life lived in ignorance. Her hands were becoming numb. She tried to move them, wriggling her fingers to encourage the flow of blood. She wanted to twist them round, to reach out and grab one hand with the other to rub the numbness away, but all she could do was form small fists as she flexed her fingers. The rope around her wrists was too tight for anything else. For now. She concentrated on her right wrist, twisting and turning it as the night sky moved above her. The rope bit deep into her skin, worrying away the upper layer of dermis, leeching fluids from her with each unrewarded struggle. The pain was acute, yet pain was good. Pain meant she was still alive. Still had a chance at escape.

The passage of the sky stopped. Orders were barked out in what she thought was French except it sounded cruder, more guttural, as if a language from another time. Hands grabbed her round the legs and arms, fingertips brushing her flesh where her clothing had ripped. Her view tipped forward ninety degrees as she was jostled and jolted upright. Hooded figures had hold of her, manoeuvring the crucifix into a standing position. They were high up in the hills here, the wind whipping around them, the clouds above them moving now to slowly reveal stars and brightening moon, obscured in part, yet full and voyeuristic. The surrounding countryside was a panorama of silhouettes, the landscape a blanket of darkness interspersed with dots of light from solitary buildings. Elizabeth could make out the farmhouse and gîte in the moonlight. She gauged the distance. They were perhaps ten to fifteen minutes from here. Less if you ran. And what about the village. Had they all come to take part? All of Pont du Diable? The village should have stood out clearly with its many lights. Yet…

A gasp escaped her lips. She had known it would be like this. It couldn't be any other way. Still, she was unprepared for what she saw. There were two more crosses, standing upright in the ground, freestanding, each cross with a man tied to it. She barely recognised Frank's face, his nose was broken, set at an unnatural angle, his mouth hung open so he could breathe. One eye was sealed shut, all puffy and dark, the other was barely open. She wondered if he could see her.

"Frank, Frank!" she shouted, desperate for him to know she was there.

She thought he hadn't heard her, that the words had been lost in the wind. She missed the movement at first, the slow raise of the head only for it fall down again. He repeated the action, stronger this time, his head remaining upright.

"Lizzie," he mumbled, too quiet for her to hear, then more forcefully, "Lizzie!"

A sad smile graced her lips. She had always hated it when he called her Lizzie. She had never told him that. She had meant to, at the beginning when they were young and in love, when it hadn't seemed worth the argument, and then it had become habit, so she had lived with it in silent resentment. Now, out here in the wilds with the wind licking at the flames around them, it was the most wonderful word to hear.

A scream pierced the night air.

"Lizzie!" Frank was shouting again, desperate for her attention. "Lizzie, what are they doing?"

She didn't dare answer.

Smoke drifted in the wind, the smell of wood burning, sweet and heady, mixed with … she thought of barbecues with friends, the one time Frank would take charge of cooking. She had been concentrating on Frank, not paying attention to what they were doing in the shadows. There was a heat to the air, embers floating past her face, catching in her clothes before dying. The screams rose the warmer it became, the flames hungrily biting at the flesh of the vagrant. Faces were hidden in shadow, figures circling the conflagration, heads bowed in prayer, palms placed together. They were the ones who had carried the wood, piling it around the crucifix. A litany was chanted to someone, something. The screams grew louder, dominating the hushed words of worship, of offering.

"Et le prochain." The next. "Le homme."

Wood was stacked at Frank's feet, bundles of twigs and branches lain on the ground. A rusty red cannister was carried through the throng, passed from hand to hand. And still the vagrant screamed. Elizabeth could only watch as the cannister was stopped in its journey.

"No," she screamed. "No, don't!" But they ignored her, splashing liquid from the cannister as it was swung back and forth over the wood pile. Fire sprang up as the first torch landed.

Elizabeth's world fell apart. Her children's faces flooded her vision. Men now. And there were memories too. Of Frank. Memories of harsh words said and kind words left unspoken. Tears fell freely across her face. She had loved Frank. Once. A long time ago. She wanted to have told him that one final time, even if the words weren't true any longer. To hug him for comfort. For familiarity. Now he had become a blur within a cloud of smoke.

"La femme!"

She could feel the villagers positioning her, trying to find the hole in the ground which would support her as her own fire laid claim to her flesh. She looked one last time to Frank, afraid of what she would see. He was waving. Waving her goodbye. His arm free. Somehow. No, he was flailing. Not waving. Reaching to free his other arm. A leg free now. And he was kicking even with the flames reaching for him. The hands supporting her vanished.

She hit the ground hard as the crucifix toppled backwards, the wood she was strapped to taking most of the force but not enough to splinter or break. People ran past her in their rush to help their brethren. She could hear shouts of alarm blending with the sounds of anguish and torment. And then a face. Moon-shaped. From the village. Fingers were working at the rope around her wrists. A knife cutting. The rope falling away from her ankles. Her hands freed.

"Go. You do not have long."

And she fled. Rolling away into the darkness amidst the confusion of the sacrifice and of Frank. Frank who was hanging from his cross still trying to free himself, trying to escape the escalating fire. Long sticks were poked at him from all angles. Catching him out of nowhere through the smoke. There was nothing she could do. Not for Frank. It was all about her from now. She didn't know if anyone had seen her but that didn't matter. Now she needed to escape. Down the darkened slope into the shadows where they might not find her. Away from the madness and her husband.

The vicar looked mournfully down the hillside as the Englishwoman tumbled towards her freedom. Conflicting voices pulled at his conscience. The men he could deal with. It was always the women he had qualms about. And the children. He replaced his hood and turned back to the gathering. He would make his peace with their god tomorrow. For now, he had played his part.

The steel was in his belly before he realised what had happened. The ground was soft beneath his knees as his body buckled and he slumped to the naked earth. The hag held him close, pushing the knife deeper into his guts. Her breath was warm in his ear, the last contact he would have with a living creature. His eyes closed gently, the whispered tendrils of a final eulogy floating in his ear.

"Au revoir, traitre. Au revoir."

~~ 14 ~~

The darkness was Elizabeth's friend even as she slipped and slithered her way down the hillside, mud plastering her hands and backside. She could hear the mob behind her but their shouts were confused.

"La femme. Ou est la femme?"

It would only be a matter of time before they spotted her. If she could make it to the gîte then there was hope. The keys to the car were on the dining table. She could picture them clearly in her head, lying where she had left them while Frank stood pointing. Frank. Poor Frank. She didn't want to think about what was happening to him. If she cried now she would never stop and that would be the end of her. There would be time enough to grieve after.

At the bottom of the hill there were bushes. Big ugly coarse bushes with needle-long thorns. Spikes tore at her flesh and clothing as she forced her way through the ragged hedgerow. She wanted to scream out loud as the bushes pierced her skin, splinters of thorn snapping from the branches and burying deep within her skin as she stumbled through to the freedom of the other side.

Her foot gave as she stepped out into moonlight. She had assumed there would be a field here. Instead she was tumbling over and over, sharp stones battering her worn body as the world twisted around her, bouncing down the steep edges of a bank. Cold, cold water engulfed her,

her skin constricting beneath her clothes. She gasped for air, rolling onto her back, thrashing like a floundering fish in the fast running water. Elizabeth staggered to her feet, slipping, then standing again. Looking wildly around as she tried to get her bearings. She was standing on the edge of a river, ankle deep, at the edge at least. She'd fallen four, maybe five feet, though it had felt like more. Now she gave praise for the dark bushes above her. There was no way her captors could see her down here. Not until they were right on top of her, at any rate. And to do that they would have to crawl through the tangle of thorns. Maybe there was a God after all.

The soft mud of the riverbed pulled at her feet as she waded across, the water playing around her ankles at first before rising to her waist the further she progressed to the middle. She held her arms out for balance, her footing uncertain, the swell of the current buffeting her bulk in the darkness. Each step was taking too long, increasing the opportunity for them to discover her. Even as she got closer to the other bank, the waters becoming shallower, she knew she wasn't moving quickly enough.

They spotted her as she climbed up the far side bank.

"La, la!" The shout rang out into the night.

Wet, battered and bruised, Elizabeth started running across the open field praying her pursuers would be halted by the hedge. Stumbling and tripping she edged closer to the gîte. Each footstep became heavier as claggy earth collected around the soles of her feet. The cloying mud gave way to the compacted soil of the farmyard. It was then she looked behind to see if they were following. She wished she hadn't. Two fires burned brightly on the crest of the hill. Elizabeth sank to her knees, breathing deeply, knowing if she stopped now that would be it, there would be no more strength to continue. In the distance she could hear more shouting. She swallowed hard and pressed on.

The door to the gîte had been left wide open. There was no need for security. Every last person had made their way to the hilltops this evening. Yet, Elizabeth still edged nervously round the doorway, half-expecting a hooded figure to be waiting in the shadows. She would be in and out quickly. Find the car keys and run. There was no way of knowing how far away her pursuers were but they couldn't be far. Fumbling in the darkness, she felt along the wall for the light switch.

Relief flooded through her as the light flared on. The keys were on the table where she had left them, along with the knife. She thanked God that she had … that she hadn't given them to Frank instead, taking them with him where they would now be caught within the burning morass upon the hillside, a charred amalgamation of metal, plastic and flesh. Elizabeth shivered.

She hurried across the room, sweeping up the keys, gripping them as if her life depended on it. It was four steps back to the door. Probably thirty more across the farmyard to the car. From there…

A noise. They were close. The mob. The hoard. The hag. The whore. With their torches and their malevolence. Were they all there? Or had some stayed for the conflagration? Watching as pale skin turned pink, then red then black. As the weeping sores sizzled, thin wisps of steam mixing with the white smoke of the fire.

Elizabeth took four steps and stopped.

The whore.

"Nowhere to run, Madame Dixon."

Madeleine blocked her escape route, the door closed behind her. Dark wet hair clung to the fine contours of her face. Her skirt and blouse had been replaced with the drab robes the others wore, yet she still held an air of elegance, a fire in her eyes. The robes hung heavily on her, soaked with water from the river and plastered with mud from the fields. Even that hadn't brought Elizabeth enough precious minutes.

Elizabeth lashed out instinctively, ignoring the weariness in her limbs. The jagged edges of the keys raked across the dewy skin of the Madeleine's face gouging deeply. The cut wept black in the shadow of the gîte, blood seeping slowly from the freshly formed wound.

"Salope!" Madeleine hissed the word, venom dripping within the syllables.

Elizabeth swung a second time, desperate to inflict further pain, enough to force her way outside. Madeleine was ready, blocking the assault, long thin fingers grabbing the tender flesh of Elizabeth's damaged wrist. She twisted hard, enjoying the anguish on Elizabeth's face as she dug her nails into the open sores where the ropes had cut deep.

The keys fell to the floor, skittering into the shadows with a sweep of Madeleine's foot. Elizabeth clawed at Madeleine's face with her free hand to little effect. Her fingernails were worn and stubby, practicality having long usurped the vanity of youth. Each swipe became more erratic as Madeleine adjusted her grip, dictating Elizabeth's movements like some macabre marionette as she harried her deeper into the room. The floor was unfamiliar, every step backwards was uncertain, the risk of falling inherent.

And all the time the others were surely closing in. If Madeleine was here the rest could only be minutes behind.

Madeleine forced her on, back into the dining table, bending Elizabeth backwards against its lip. Crockery and cutlery clattered to the floor. Broken white shards sprayed out across the tiles. All the time Madeleine kept pressing.

She was up close to her victim now, her right hand maintaining its grip, her left reaching for the greying wattle of Elizabeth's neck. Elizabeth fought back. Blow after blow hit Madeleine's head, each one becoming weaker as Madeleine squeezed hard on Elizabeth's throat. Crescents of blood formed along her neck. Her arm flailed as the world around her darkened. Flashes of light appeared in her vision, each flare blotting out the anger and determination in Madeleine's face. Elizabeth could die now and that would be that. No one would know what had happened. None of the villagers would admit anything. She would be forgotten like the monks, a mound of earth in a village in the middle of nowhere.

Two hands were around her neck now. Choking the life from her. Elizabeth's arm left to flop free onto the table. Cold lengthy steel brushed the back of her numbing fingers. Her befuddled brain functioned without her knowledge, fingers curling, grasping the knife, swinging one last futile time.

"Cawk, cawk."

The noise came from Madeleine, confusion replacing confidence. A thick fountain of blood spurted from her neck. Her mouth opened and closed, fishlike, pointlessly sucking in air even as her body began to convulse. Fingers released their grip on Elizabeth, hands floundering for the knife stuck deep into the side of her windpipe as she sank to her knees.

And somewhere in the darkness an old woman howled in rage.

~~ 15 ~~

The hag was seething with fury at the window, her features a contorted mess of sorrow and apoplexy framed by a backdrop of orange. Her followers stood with her, torches in hand.

"Brûle le gîte," she said.

Windows shattered as the acolytes followed their orders. Burn the gîte. Burn it down. Kill the bitch. Kill her now!

Flaming wood landed inside the gîte. Sparks caught everywhere; eager all-consuming tongues of fire licked hungrily at the interior. The curtains caught quickest, hot streaks of flame running up the length of the heavy fabric. Globules of fire dripped on to the floor where the drapes had been interwoven with cheap polyester.

Elizabeth drifted between consciousness.

The room was a blur of smoke and flame. Direction had no meaning. It took her precious seconds to understand the difference between ceiling and floor. Elizabeth gripped the edge of the table, using it for reassurance and navigation.

Madeleine's corpse was warm at her feet, a grim landmark in a room composed of shades. The exit would be directly ahead. Four steps once more.

One.

Her heel caught the soft flesh of Madeleine's hand. For a second she thought there was a twitch, a grab made for her ankle seeking to drag her down to the ground.

Two. Three.

Panicked steps away from the lifeless body. Heartbeat racing. Realisation dawning that dead is dead.

Four.

A wall. Smooth and cool even as the fires burn in the room behind. Step left. Hands palm out against the surface of the wall. Step left. Step left. Wood.

Locked. It was locked. The whore had locked it. Elizabeth raged at the door. Pulling at the door handle. Shaking it. Both hands gripping the metal ring, feet planted to the floor, leaning back with all her weight to the point at which she thought the wounds on her wrist would split open. She collapsed backwards into the room, the floor slamming into her back, forcing the air from her lungs.

The fire was raging now across the downstairs. Instinct drove her to move. Forced her up on to uncertain feet. Stagger left. Flames. Right. More flames. Forward. The whore. The table. Distant glimpses of demons in the smoke watching from the peripheries. Or was it the villagers through scantly glimpsed windows.

Her head felt light, an unexpected feeling of euphoria creeping up on her as the oxygen was sucked from the room. The table was real though. An island of orientation in the midst of the maelstrom. Elizabeth used her hands to guide her round its edges. Her options were reducing as each second passed, as each fibre in the building caught fire. The walls were alive, warping and writhing with the heat, preventing her getting anywhere near the windows and the fresh air outside. The kitchen was a cauldron of toxins and smoke as the plastics and chemicals of the fridge burned with gusto.

She placed a bloodied fist on the newel of the stairs. Hand over hand she clawed her way up the stairs, using the bannister to prevent herself from collapsing, ascending from one hell to another. Three quarters of the way up the stairway started to sway. She ran, panic driving her forward, diving to the ground as the stairs collapsed behind her as she crested the final step. She spun round, squirming on her belly to look down into the conflagration. Madeleine looked back at her from the ground, dead-eyed and unmoving. Fire caught her long black hair, running along its length far quicker than Elizabeth would have thought possible. She watched longer than she meant to, only turning away in disgust as the Frenchwoman's scalp began to blister and peel.

Around her, smoke began to rise from the floorboards. How long did she have before the whole room collapsed into the fires below? She thought back to her dream. The hag in the window. Except that was in her head.

Elizabeth rushed across the room, bashing into the bath in her haste, ignoring the pain as she hurried towards the bed. She tore at the sheets, dragging them free and running with them to the window. If she could tie them to something maybe she could lower herself down before the hoard realised what was happening. She pushed at the glass, all steamed up, pivoting the window open to allow the fresh breeze to vent into the room. Cold air kissed her cheek, a promise of hope and freedom. She could do this. She could actually escape. She just had to…

Elizabeth let the sheets fall to the floor.

There was to be no dash to freedom. No miraculous leap into the darkness to escape the clutches of evil. There was only death and failure.

They were waiting for her. All of them. The hag at their forefront looking up knowingly at Elizabeth as she had at so many before her, and as she would at others yet to come. This is how things were round here. How they had always been.

So this was where it would end. In a farmhouse in a foreign country with no one to hold her. To tell her everything would be all right even if it were not true.

Elizabeth shuffled across the room, lost, heavy footsteps leading her on. She stopped. There was an obstacle in her way. The smooth cold edges of the bath. Unthinking, she clambered inside, slumping down into its depths. The taps gave easily, twisting at the behest of her weary fingers. The pipes gurgled and chuntered as they pulled water up through the plumbing.

The hag leered at Elizabeth lying bereft in the bath. The angle of the window reflected her grizzled features on to the heat-warped glass. A trick of the light, of refraction, of science. It had to be. Even now Elizabeth couldn't admit that magic might exist. Not this magic.

Elizabeth sank deeper into her grave, desperate for the hag not to be the last thing she saw. That was one small victory she would have. She closed her eyes, darkness descending, and curled up foetus-like within the comfort of the water, thinking of her children and happier times. The boys playing together, at school, on holidays, getting older, becoming men. Just the two of them. She cried tears as water flowed into the bath, some of joy, some of regret.

Oh so many tears. Tears which comforted and tears as hot as the raging fire in the walls. Tears which were decades overdue spilling forth and mingling with the water. She cried until she couldn't cry anymore. And that was how Elizabeth Dixon passed from this world.

Lightning Source UK Ltd.
Milton Keynes UK
UKHW011943080420
361516UK00001B/23